L M Montgomery's

Anne *of* Green Gables

Retold by Rachel Delahaye

Illustrated by Dave Williams

RISING STARS

ISBN: 9781510445062

Text © 2019 Rachel Delahaye
Illustrations, design and layout © 2019 Rising Stars UK Ltd
First published in 2019 by Rising Stars UK Ltd

Rising Stars UK Ltd, part of Hodder Education Group
An Hachette UK Company
Carmelite House 50 Victoria Embankment London EC4Y 0DZ

www.risingstars-uk.com

Impression number 10 9 8 7 6 5 4 3 2 1
Year 2023 2022 2021 2020 2019

Author: Rachel Delahaye
Series Editor: Sasha Morton
Senior Publisher: Helen Parker
Illustrator: Giada Gatti and Dave Williams/Bright Group International
Editorial Consultant: Pauline Allen
Design concept: Helen Townson
Page layout: Steve Evans
Editorial Manager: Hamish Baxter

With thanks to the schools that took part in the development of Reading Planet KS2, including: Ancaster CE Primary School, Ancaster; Downsway Primary School, Reading; Ferry Lane Primary School, London; Foxborough Primary School, Slough; Griffin Park Primary School, Blackburn; St Barnabas CE First & Middle School, Pershore; Tranmoor Primary School, Doncaster; and Wilton CE Primary School, Wilton.

A catalogue record for this title is available from the British Library.

Printed in India

Orders: Please contact Bookpoint Ltd, 130 Park Drive, Milton Park, Abingdon, Oxon OX14 4SE. Telephone: (44) 01235 400555. Email: primary@bookpoint.co.uk.

Contents

Anne of Green Gables

with scenes to act out!

ACT IT OUT! – Character List

Anne Shirley

Anne is an orphan who comes
to live with the Cuthberts.

Marilla Cuthbert

Marilla has never
been married.
She lives with her
brother, Matthew.

Matthew Cuthbert

Matthew has never married and
lives with Marilla on their farm,
Green Gables.

Rachel Lynde

Rachel is Marilla's friend and busybody neighbour.

Diana Barry

Diana is Anne's age and lives near Green Gables.

Gilbert Blythe

Gilbert is an intelligent boy who goes to the same school as Anne and Diana.

A note on the location: This story is set on Prince Edward Island in Canada. If you're ever lucky enough to go there, you could visit the house Green Gables is based on, as well as an Anne of Green Gables shop and museum.

1

Waiting at the Train Station

"Are you serious, Marilla?" Rachel Lynde demanded.

Marilla nodded and crossed her arms. Rachel considered herself to be an expert in everything – including taking in orphans.

"What on earth put such an idea in your head!" Rachel spluttered. "If you had asked my advice first, I would have told you not to even think of it."

Marilla smiled thinly. Rachel was a neighbour and a friend, but she was also the nosiest busybody in the town of Avonlea.

"There's a risk in everything we do in this world, Rachel. We've made up our minds."

Rachel shook her head pityingly. "Do you remember the case of an orphan girl who poisoned her adoptive family's well?"

"We're not getting a girl," Marilla said firmly. "We're getting a boy to help Matthew with the farm work."

At that very moment, Matthew was at the train station, waiting to collect the orphan boy who would join the quiet life he and his sister, Marilla, shared at Green Gables farm. What could possibly go wrong?

ACT IT OUT!

Outside the station, Anne is waiting. Matthew sees her and then looks around.

Anne: Are you Mr Matthew Cuthbert?

Matthew stops and nods slowly.

Anne: Phew! I was beginning to think you weren't coming. I had decided to climb up that big cherry tree and wait for you until morning. Wouldn't it be lovely to sleep in a cherry tree in the moonshine?

Matthew: *(Nervously)* Yes, well, sorry I was late.

Anne and Matthew climb into a horse-drawn cart. Anne wriggles with excitement.

Anne: It seems so wonderful that I'm going to live with you. I've never belonged to anyone before. Isn't that cherry tree beautiful? What does it remind you of with the flowers all lacy and white?

Matthew: Well, I don't know.

Anne:	A bride of course! With a white misty veil. I think this must be the bloomiest place in all Canada. Am I talking too much?
Matthew:	You can talk as much as you like. I don't mind.
Anne:	Oh good. People laugh at me because I use big words, but if you have big ideas you need big words, don't you?
Matthew:	Makes sense.
Anne:	This is a dream come true! Dreams don't come true very often, do they? Right now, I am perfectly happy. No, not perfectly … What colour would you call my hair?
Matthew:	Red.
Anne:	And that is why I can never be perfectly happy. Red hair will be my lifelong sorrow. Look Mr Cuthbert, a tunnel of blossoming apple trees! What is this place called?
Matthew:	The Avenue.
Anne:	There's no feeling in a name like that. They should call it – let me see – the 'White Way of Delight'. And that pond over there shall be the Lake of Shining Waters.
Matthew:	It's called the Barry's Pond because Mr Barry lives up there in that house. He has a daughter your age called Diana.
Anne:	*(Dreamily)* Diana of the Lake of Shining Waters … Is that Green Gables over there?

Matthew: You guessed it.

Anne: Do you know, I've pinched myself so many times I've bruised my arm? I had a horrible feeling that it was all a dream. But as soon as I saw Green Gables I just felt like it was home.

2

A New Face

When Rachel had gone, Marilla made herself busy. She set the table for tea, and then stood outside on the porch to wait. Green Gables had always been a quiet household – but now it was perfectly silent, as if the house was waiting for something to happen.

Horse hooves clip-clopped on the road beyond the farm. They were here! Quickly, Marilla patted the creases from her dress and smoothed her hair. The horse and cart trundled up the lane. Was Matthew smiling? They had barely come to a stop when a child leaped from the buggy and landed at her feet. A girl, with a freckled face and two long braids of bright red hair.

ACT IT OUT!

Marilla: Matthew Cuthbert! Who is that? Where's the boy?

Matthew: There was just a girl. I couldn't leave her there.

Marilla and Matthew look at Anne. Anne realises something is wrong.

Anne: Oh! You don't want me! I knew it was too good to be true. This is the most tragic thing that has ever happened to me!

Marilla: *(Sharply)* Come on, settle down now. Tell me your name.

Anne: Can you call me Cordelia? It's such a pretty name.

Marilla: No more nonsense. What is your real name?

Anne: Boring Anne Shirley. But if you are going to call me Anne, could you spell it with an 'e' at the end? It sounds so much more sophisticated.

Marilla: Very well, Anne with an 'e'. I'm sorry, but we have no use for a girl.

Anne: *(To Matthew)* Why didn't you just leave me at the station if you didn't want me? If I hadn't seen the White Way of Delight and the Lake of Shining Waters it wouldn't be so hard.

Marilla: *(To Matthew)* What is she talking about?

Matthew:	Just some conversation we had on the road …
Marilla:	We'll sort out this mess in the morning. Come and eat something.
Anne:	I can't eat when I'm in the depths of despair! Can you imagine being in the depths of despair, Miss Cuthbert?
Matthew:	Please have a little something to eat now, won't you, Anne?

After Anne had indulged Matthew by having some tea, despite being in the depths of despair, she followed Marilla up the stairs to her room and sorrowfully climbed into bed.

Marilla looked at the young girl with her tear-stained cheeks. Poor thing. Still, there was no point in being too soft, she told herself.

"Good night, Anne."

"How can you call it a good night when it might be the worst I've ever had!" Anne exclaimed tearfully.

Marilla didn't know what to say, so she carefully closed the door and went down to the kitchen. Matthew looked at her glumly.

"It seems a pity to send her back," he said.

"What good would she be to us?"

Matthew, who didn't usually say much, shifted in his chair and coughed.

"We might be some good to her," he mumbled. "She's an interesting thing. You should have heard her talking on the journey home …"

"Matthew Cuthbert!" Marilla exclaimed. "I have noticed for myself that the girl can talk. I don't like children who have so much to say. No, she's got to go back to the orphanage and that's that."

3

No Returns

Next morning, Anne tried hard to be brave – sitting at breakfast with her back straight and her hair brushed. She noticed Matthew looked sad, and smiled brightly.

"The world doesn't seem such a howling wilderness as it did last night," she declared. "All mornings are interesting, don't you think? You don't know what's going to happen throughout the day. There's so much scope for imagination—"

"For goodness' sake, you chatter on too much!" Marilla scolded.

Because Anne was desperate to please Marilla, she didn't say another word. After breakfast, Marilla got the horse and cart ready, and Anne climbed aboard silently. With a flick of the reins, the buggy rolled down the path and out of Green Gables. Marilla looked back to see Matthew shaking his head sadly. He had taken such a shine to her ... but no, they would go to Mrs Spencer. Her brother ran the orphanage on the mainland and she would sort it all out.

Anne, still not talking, stared blankly ahead as they rolled back down the country lane. It made Marilla feel uncomfortable. She had to admit, she was confused by this strange girl who lived far away in her own imagination.

"Why don't you tell me about yourself to pass the time," she suggested.

Anne breathed a sigh of relief at being able to talk again, and the story of her childhood tumbled out. She was

just three months old when her parents had died of fever. She was taken in by a local woman, who then passed her to another woman who had three sets of twins that Anne was made to look after. After that, she was put in the children's home.

"Oh look!" Anne gasped. As the country road met the coast, the view of the ocean opened up before them. "Isn't the sea wonderful? Aren't those gulls splendid? Wouldn't it be nice to swoop down over the blue water every day?"

Marilla said nothing, but she was moved by Anne's story. The little girl had already been through so much.

When they reached Mrs Spencer, Marilla explained the problem – they had clearly asked for an orphan boy, and would the orphanage take her back?

"Actually, that won't be necessary," Mrs Spencer said brightly. "Mrs Blewett was here yesterday, asking for a girl to help her at home. Anne is used to working with children. She will be perfect! And look, here comes Mrs Blewett now!"

Mrs Blewett had a reputation as a disagreeable woman with a fierce temper. She looked Anne up and down as if she were inspecting a farm animal.

"You'll do," the woman said flatly. "But I'll expect you to earn your keep. I've got a houseful of children and I'm worn out with the new baby. You can come with me right now."

The colour drained from Anne's face. Marilla's heart skipped a sudden beat. She knew that Anne was too sensitive and sweet for a life with the mean-spirited Mrs Blewett. "Now wait a moment," Marilla interrupted. "I didn't say we had absolutely decided to give her back, and I can't make a decision without talking to Matthew."

Anne felt hope spread through her like warm water. As they walked back to the buggy, she asked, "Miss Cuthbert, did you really say I can stay? Or did I just imagine you did?"

"I think you ought to control that imagination of yours, Anne," replied Marilla, with a twitch of a smile.

That night, Marilla and Matthew stayed up late talking about Anne.

"I've got used to the idea of keeping her," Marilla said. Matthew's face lit up. "I'll train her to be useful. You're not to be soft on her, Matthew. If she stays, we do it my way."

"Anything you say, Marilla." A smile tugged at the corners of his mouth. "I reckon she'll do anything you ask if you get her to love you."

Marilla raised an eyebrow – what did he know about bringing up girls!

They told Anne the next morning. Tears sprung from her eyes.

"I'm as glad as glad can be. I'm more than glad. I'm so happy! Shall I call you Aunt Marilla? I've never had any relations. It would make me feel like I belonged."

"No, you'll call me plain Marilla."

Marilla did not believe in spoiling children, and explained exactly how she wanted Anne to behave. She was to be obedient and speak respectfully, and help with all the household chores.

When Marilla had finished explaining, Anne went to her room to unpack her meagre belongings. But in no time, she got carried away with her imagination, dreaming that she was Lady Cordelia living in a luxurious palace. She danced up to the mirror on the wall and met a face with freckles and green eyes.

"You're only Anne of Green Gables," she sighed. "But it's a million times better than being Anne of Nowhere, isn't it?"

4

The Unfairness of Insults

Anne wanted to get to know everything about Green Gables. She named the cherry blossom tree outside her window 'Snow Queen'. She explored the orchard, the woodland and the hollow, where there was a spring and a stream. She chatted about her discoveries in great detail, mainly to Matthew, who loved hearing her talk.

It wasn't long before Rachel Lynde came to meet the Cuthberts' new arrival. Anne was playing in the orchard when she arrived, giving Rachel a chance to let Marilla know her feelings.

"I've heard all about it, Marilla. A girl? Couldn't you have sent her back?" she tutted.

"We decided not to," said Marilla. "She's a bright little thing."

"Bright? You hardly know anything about her … but I don't want to worry you, Marilla."

Marilla smiled patiently and called Anne in from the garden.

"Anne, this is Rachel Lynde."

Anne curtseyed. The woman's face twisted into a strange, mocking smile.

ACT IT OUT!

Rachel: Well, they didn't pick you for your looks! (*To Marilla*) She's so scrawny and plain. Oh my goodness, those freckles. And her hair is as red as carrots!

Anne is instantly enraged.

Anne: (*To Rachel*) How dare you say I'm scrawny and that my hair is like carrots! You are a rude, unkind woman. I hate you – I hate you – I hate you!

Marilla: Anne Shirley!

Anne: (*To Rachel*) How would you feel if someone said you were old and wrinkly?

Anne storms out.

Rachel: (*Calmly*) She's the kind of child that will poison your drinking water, Marilla.

Rachel leaves. Anne returns.

Anne: She had no right to say that to me, Marilla.

Marilla: Rachel is a friend and an adult. You will apologise.

Anne: No! You can lock me in a dungeon with snakes and toads, but I will not ask Mrs Lynde to forgive me.

Marilla:	We don't have many damp dungeons in Avonlea, Anne, but you'll go to your room and stay there until you say sorry.
Anne:	I'll have to stay there forever then!

Anne didn't come down for dinner that evening, or the next morning. Marilla left food by her bedroom door, but Anne was so enraged that she could hardly eat a thing. Marilla was just as stubborn. Matthew waited until his sister had gone out and crept upstairs to Anne's room. He found her staring out of the window.

"You've been up here a mighty long time," he said, in his quiet way.

"I imagine things to pass the time."

"Anne, Marilla won't back down. Why don't you just get this apology over and done with? It's lonely downstairs without you."

Anne looked at Matthew. He was a kind and wonderful man – a kindred spirit. She didn't want to let him down.

"Alright. I'd do anything for you, Matthew."

"Good. But don't tell Marilla we talked. She doesn't want me interfering."

Anne grinned. "Wild horses won't drag our secret from me."

5

Making Friends

ACT IT OUT!

Rachel is on a chair on her porch. Marilla and Anne approach.

Marilla: Rachel, Anne has something to say.

Anne clasps her hands.

Anne: *(Emotionally)* Every word you said is true. I am scrawny and freckly, and my hair is as red as carrots. Please forgive me. If you refuse, it will be my lifelong sorrow.

Rachel: *(Surprised)* Of course I forgive you. I like to speak my mind, that's all. Don't worry about your terribly red hair, dear. It might darken to a beautiful auburn over time.

Anne: Oh, Mrs Lynde, you fill me with hope.

Anne skips down the garden.

Rachel: Well, Marilla. Anne is an odd little thing, but on the whole ... I kind of like her.

"I apologised pretty well, didn't I?" Anne said brightly, on the way back to Green Gables.

"You certainly did," Marilla said, trying not to laugh. "But from now on, you'll control your temper."

"When people make fun of my hair I can't help it – it just makes me boil over."

Anne looked up at the sky. "Aren't the stars clear tonight? If you could live in a star, which one would it be? I'd like that big clear one over there."

Marilla felt the orphan girl's hand slip into hers. It took her by surprise, as she was unused to physical affection. Very carefully, she folded her fingers around the little hand and held it, all the way home.

A few days later, Marilla spread three dresses out on Anne's bed. She had made them herself, using hard-wearing material and a sensible design.

"How do you like these, Anne?"

"I can imagine I like them," Anne shrugged. "They're not very pretty."

"I thought, after wearing those terrible dresses from the orphanage, you would be grateful," Marilla said, sharply. She was a little hurt.

"I am grateful. I just dream of a dress with puffed sleeves. That would give me such a thrill!"

Marilla, who had never worn a fancy dress in her life, was not impressed with Anne's fashion dreams. "Plain is best. Now Anne, I am going to see Mrs Barry. Why don't you come with me and meet her daughter, Diana?"

Anne's hands clasped together in joy. A friend to play with!

"Diana of the Lake of Shining Waters is going to be my best friend …" She stopped, struck by a terrible thought. "What if she doesn't like me?"

Marilla tutted. "It's her mother you have to impress. If she doesn't like you, it doesn't matter what Diana thinks."

"Oh Marilla, I'm frightened," Anne said, tears springing from her eyes. "If she didn't like me, it would be the most tragic disappointment of my life!"

"Don't get into a fluster," Marilla tutted, as she pinned her most precious possession – an amethyst brooch – onto her coat. "And I do wish you wouldn't use such long words!"

6

Making Promises

The Barry household was only a short walk from Green Gables, but Anne trembled with nervous excitement all the way there.

Mrs Barry had dark hair, dark eyes and a stern face. When she called Diana to come forward to welcome their visitors, Anne thought her heart might burst out of her chest.

Diana looked just like her mother, apart from the set of her face, which was bright and cheerful. Anne and Diana smiled shyly at each other.

"Diana, why don't you take Anne into the garden?" Mrs Barry suggested.

The two girls walked silently in the beautiful evening light, not knowing what to say. As the late sun filtered through the trees and the bees hummed drowsily, Anne was suddenly overcome with emotion.

ACT IT OUT!

Anne: Oh Diana, do you think you can like me enough to be my best friend?

Diana: *(Laughing)* I guess so.

Anne: Will you swear to be my friend forever and ever?

Diana: *(Shocked)* Anne! Swearing is bad.

Anne: Swearing means promising something. We must join hands.

Anne and Diana face each other and hold hands.

Anne: I solemnly swear to be faithful to my best friend, Diana Barry, for as long as the sun and the moon shall endure. Now, you say it.

Diana: I solemnly swear to be faithful to my best friend, Anne Shirley, for as long as the sun and the moon shall endure.

Anne and Diana grin at each other.

Diana: You're so funny, Anne. I'm glad you've come to Avonlea.

One late August evening, Diana had given Anne some thrilling news. She came home overflowing with excitement. Marilla watched from the kitchen window as Anne jumped up and down in front of Matthew, waving her hands theatrically. Matthew stopped his work and listened to every word. Then

Anne flew into the house with her red braids dancing behind her.

"Oh, Marilla," she panted. "There's a school picnic next week. There's going to be ice-cream. Ice-cream! Can I go?"

"You were supposed to be home at two o'clock," Marilla tutted.

"Oh, I know. But Diana and I had such fun playing in nature, and then I had to tell Matthew, because he's

such a good listener, and … oh please, Marilla!" Anne wrapped her arms around Marilla and squeezed her tightly.

"Enough of that now." Secretly, Anne's affection made her very happy, but Marilla felt it was important to keep her enthusiasm under control. "Now, get out your sewing and have it done before teatime."

Even though she hated sewing, being Anne of Green Gables was the best thing in the world. And Anne of Green Gables was going to try ice-cream for the very first time!

But on the afternoon of the picnic, Marilla entered Anne's room with a troubled face.

ACT IT OUT!

Marilla: Anne, have you seen my amethyst brooch?

Anne: *(Guiltily)* I did see it on your pin cushion. I picked it up to look at it, but I put it right back.

Marilla: You will stay in your room until you confess!

Anne: But the picnic is this afternoon!

Marilla: You'll be going nowhere until you confess.

Anne suddenly thinks of something.

Anne: I was pretending to be Lady Cordelia Fitzgerald. I put it on and went for a walk by the lake, and it slipped off and sank – all purply-sparkling – to the bottom.

Marilla: Anne Shirley, you are the wickedest girl I ever heard of. As your punishment, you will not be going to that picnic.

Anne: Please, Marilla. Punish me any other way, but not that.

Matthew: *(Off-stage)* Marilla!

Marilla tuts and leaves. She soon returns, holding the brooch.

Marilla: Matthew found the brooch caught in my shawl. Why did you confess to taking it?

Anne: Because you told me to. I made the confession as interesting as I could.

Marilla: Anne, I'll forgive you for lying, if you forgive me for not trusting you. Now, let's get you ready for the picnic.

7

Meeting People

When the new term started, Anne and Diana walked together every day to Avonlea school. It was a pretty white building next to a stream, where the children placed their bottles of milk to keep them cool until lunchtime. As far as Anne was concerned, it was perfect.

Most of the class didn't know what to make of the new girl, who wore flowers in her hair and used unusual words, but they were welcoming. Diana had warned Anne about some of the boys, and how they teased the girls endlessly – especially Gilbert Blythe. That became clear right away when Anne saw him pin Ruby's long braid to the back of her chair. When Gilbert saw Anne watching, he wasn't ashamed – he winked at her!

ACT IT OUT!

Diana: That's Gilbert over there. He's really smart.

Anne: He may be smart, but he's too confident.

Gilbert runs across the room and tugs Anne's hair.

Gilbert: Carrots! Carrots!

Anne: *(Flaring)* How dare you! You mean, hateful boy!

Anne gets up and cracks her writing slate over Gilbert's head.

Diana: *(Gasps)* Anne! You'll be in trouble now.

Mr Phillips, the teacher, stood threateningly before Anne's desk. Gilbert leaped up while rubbing his head remorsefully.

"It was my fault, I teased her!" he protested, but it was no good.

Anne was made to write 'Anne Shirley has a very bad temper' on the blackboard and stand underneath it. She refused to cry. She stood tall and looked straight ahead. Gilbert tried hard to get her attention. No way! She was never going to speak to him again. Why did people think it was acceptable to draw attention to her red hair?

"Anne Shirley, as you have acted like one of the boys, you'll be sitting next to Gilbert from now on," Mr Phillips announced.

Anne flounced into the chair next to Gilbert and lay her head on the desk. This was the worst day ever. Gilbert tried to slip a note under her arm, but Anne pushed it to the floor. When school was over, she ran from the classroom in a humiliated rage.

"Gilbert makes fun of all the girls," Diana said, catching up with her friend.

"He has hurt my feelings, Diana," Anne said, stubbornly. "And I will not speak to him or sit with him ever again."

Diana gasped. "But Mr Phillips said you have to sit next to Gilbert."

"I won't go back to school, then," Anne said, matter-of-factly.

"Don't do this. I'll miss you terribly, Anne!" Diana wailed.

"I'd do almost anything in the world for you, Diana," Anne said. "But I can't do this."

8

Tea for Two

On the advice of Rachel Lynde, who didn't believe girls should sit with boys, Marilla let Anne stay home. She would go back to school when she ran out of stubbornness.

But Anne remained stubborn throughout September and into October. When the trees changed colour, Anne decorated her room with their gold and red leaves. She continued to do her schoolwork at home, but Anne missed Diana desperately. One day, Marilla found her weeping.

"Whatever is the matter, Anne?"

"I love Diana so much, Marilla. I cannot live without her. And one day, she'll get married and will leave me ... I will be her bridesmaid with a lovely dress with puffed sleeves, but beneath my smile there will be a breaking heart ..."

What a drama Anne was inventing! Marilla laughed so loudly that Matthew heard it from the yard.

"Perhaps this will make you feel better," Marilla said. "I'm going into town this afternoon. While I'm gone, you may invite Diana over for tea."

"Oh Marilla! I've longed for that very thing. Can I use the rose-decorated tea set?"

"No, but there's a bottle of my home-made raspberry cordial on the shelf in the kitchen. You can have some as a treat."

The girls dressed up for the occasion, wearing their best dresses and hats. They shook hands like adults on the doorstep and then ran inside to the tea table, where they tucked into their cakes.

ACT IT OUT!

Diana: I have to sit next to Gertie Pye now and I hate it, Anne. Did I tell you that Sam Boulter was cheeky in class and Gilbert Blythe—

Anne: I don't want to talk about that boy, Diana. Let's try some of Marilla's raspberry cordial!

Anne runs to the kitchen and brings back a bottle of pink liquid. She pours two glasses. Diana gulps.

Diana: I didn't know raspberry cordial was so delicious!

Anne: Have as much as you want. I'm going to fetch us some more cakes!

Anne leaves. Diana keeps drinking. Anne returns.

Diana: *(Giggling)* This is the nicest drink I ever drank!

Anne: Yes, Marilla is a wonderful cook. She's been trying to teach me to bake, but I start thinking up stories and … and I get so carried away—

Diana stands up, wobbling.

Diana: Oh, Anne. I feel sick.

Anne: Lie down. You'll feel better in a minute.

Diana: I really have to go home.

Diana stumbles out. Anne is bewildered.

The next day, Marilla had sent Anne to fetch something from Rachel Lynde's house. But in no time at all, Anne was running back up the path, wailing.

"Whatever has gone wrong now?" Marilla demanded.

"Mrs Lynde saw Mrs Barry. She says I made Diana ill and Diana is never allowed to play with me again!"

Marilla looked startled. "What on earth did you give her?"

"Just your raspberry cordial …"

Marilla marched into the pantry. She spotted the cordial bottle with not a drop left in it, and the empty cake plate. The girls had eaten the lot! With so much sugar inside her, it was no wonder Diana was sick. It hardly seemed Anne's fault if Diana had a lack of self-control, but Anne did seem to have a knack of getting into trouble. "Don't cry, Anne."

"I can't not cry," Anne sobbed. "My heart is broken!"

9

Goodbyes and Hellos

Marilla tried to smooth things over with Mrs Barry, but Mrs Barry refused to back down. Anne then tried to talk to her, too, but her big words and dramatic speeches seemed to make Mrs Barry angrier.

"You are not fit to be Diana's friend," she said, cruelly. "Go home."

Anne returned home heartbroken. If she was ever going to see Diana again, there was only one thing left to do. The following Monday morning, Anne made an announcement.

"I am going back to school. At least I will be able to see Diana there."

"Fine, but I don't wish to hear of any more bad behaviour," Marilla said sternly.

"I will try to be a model student."

Anne wasn't expecting much of a welcome back, but the class at Avonlea school had missed her imagination and lively conversation. They gave her presents of flowers, poems and new pencils. Also sitting on her desk was a gift of a single strawberry apple. There was only one orchard in Avonlea that grew strawberry apples, and it belonged to Gilbert Blythe's family. Anne made a point of holding the apple high in the air and dropping it onto the floor, where it bruised and rolled away.

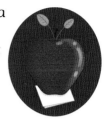

There was also a note from Diana.

Dear Anne,
Mother says I'm not to speak to you, even in school.
I love you as much as ever. I miss you terribly.
Your true friend,
Diana

Days passed, and Anne behaved herself and studied hard. She had a new goal – she was not going to come second to Gilbert Blythe in any of their lessons. Soon enough, a rivalry between the two of them began.

Anne and Gilbert's names were written up on the blackboard regularly for earning the best grades. And while Gilbert politely congratulated Anne every time she beat him at English, she would have preferred him to be upset, just as she was whenever he beat her at maths.

10

Anne to the Rescue!

One afternoon, Marilla and Rachel went off to a women's meeting in Charlottetown. They would be gone overnight, so for once Anne and Matthew had the house to themselves.

By the light of the fire, Matthew read on the sofa while Anne tried to study her maths, determined to beat Gilbert on their next test.

Suddenly, their peaceful evening was interrupted by the sound of heavy footsteps outside. Someone was in a hurry. The kitchen door flew open and there stood Diana, out of breath, with wild eyes.

ACT IT OUT!

Diana: Help! Anne! Come quick. My little sister is sick. The babysitter doesn't have a clue what to do, and my mother and father are out!

Matthew: I'll call for the doctor.

Diana: The doctor is out of town, too. The baby is coughing and can't breathe. I don't know what to do!

Anne: That sounds like croup. I worked for a family whose children had croup all the time, so I know exactly what to do.

The girls grab each other's hands and run. They burst into the Barry household. Anne rushes to the small coughing child on the sofa.

Anne: It's croup all right. Boil some water and put some wood in the stove. I'll find some syrup. Don't worry, Diana. I'm here.

Anne and Diana stayed up all night with Minnie May. Eventually, the coughing stopped and Minnie May slept. It was three o'clock in the morning when Matthew arrived with a doctor he'd fetched from Spencervale. Anne stepped forward to speak.

"When we ran out of syrup, I was worried she might die. You will have to imagine my relief when she got better, because I can't express it in words."

The doctor listened to her explanation with interest. Although he didn't say much then, he told Mr and Mrs Barry exactly what he thought of Anne the next day. He said: "That little red-haired girl is as smart as they come. She saved your baby's life."

With Minnie May safe, Anne and Matthew returned home with the sun rising over the cold, glistening fields.

"I'm so glad I live in a world where there are white frosts, don't you?" Anne yawned.

"You just go right to bed now, Anne. There'll be no school for you tomorrow."

Anne slept like a log and when she woke, Marilla was waiting for her.

ACT IT OUT!

Anne: *(Yawning)* Good morning, Marilla.

Marilla: Good afternoon, more like. *(Pauses)* Anne, Diana's mother came earlier, while you were sleeping. She would like to apologise.

Anne: Can I go right away?

Marilla: Yes, yes, run along.

Marilla and Matthew sit, drinking tea and smiling. Anne rushes back.

Anne: Marilla, I am perfectly happy – yes, despite my red hair. Tomorrow is Diana's birthday, and I've been invited to go to a concert and stay the night.

| **Marilla:** | You can calm down, because you're not going to a concert. Concerts are for adults. |

Anne stamps out.

| **Matthew:** | Well now Marilla, I think you should let Anne go. |
| **Marilla:** | You'd let her go to the moon if she asked. But given that she saved little Minnie May, I guess it won't hurt just this once. |

After school the following day, everyone celebrated Diana's birthday with an 'elegant tea'. Then, along with Diana's cousins, they piled onto a shiny, wooden sleigh and rode across the snow to the Avonlea concert. It was magical! Choirs sang and the residents of Avonlea performed their talents on stage. Gilbert Blythe read out a poem, which Anne made a particular point of not listening to. When they got home, the girls stayed up giggling and talking about all the acts, yet Anne still blankly refused to even speak Gilbert Blythe's name.

11

A Year Passes in Avonlea

"Do you know what day it is, Marilla?" Anne asked as she gazed through the kitchen window at the spring blossoms outside.

"I can't say I do."

"It's been a year since I came to Green Gables! A whole year, and I've been so happy," Anne said.

Although she didn't say so, in truth Marilla felt the same. She couldn't remember the quiet life she and Matthew led before Anne came along – and she didn't want to.

Over the following months, Anne helped around the house and studied hard at school. She also steadfastly ignored Gilbert Blythe, despite his attempts to be friendly. At the end of June, and the school year, Mr Phillips finished teaching at Avonlea school and there was a rumour that his replacement was going to be a woman!

Rachel Lynde thought female teachers were a terrible idea and Marilla was uncertain, but Anne thought it was tremendously exciting. One day, she hoped to be a teacher too! She could hardly wait for the holidays to be over and for school to begin again.

But she would have to wait a long time. After a disastrous game of 'dare' – where Anne walked on the ridgepole of a roof, fell and broke her ankle – the doctor prescribed seven weeks' rest. This was terrible in so many ways! She would miss the first day back at Avonlea school, and she would be the last to meet the new teacher. Worse still, Gilbert would get ahead of her in class.

Her school friends visited regularly with gifts and gossip. Diana told her all about Miss Muriel Stacy, the new teacher, and how she took them to the woods to study nature. Anne just knew Miss Stacy was going to be a kindred spirit!

It was October when Anne was well enough to go back to school. And she had been right about Miss Stacy – she was kind and generous, and her lessons were exciting.

"I love her with my whole heart," she told Marilla. "When she pronounces my name, I know she's spelling it with an 'e'. She says I write the best write-ups of our field trips. And do you want to know the best thing? She says Avonlea school can hold a concert in the school hall on Christmas night to raise money for a school flag."

Anne talked non-stop with excitement, and when she had finished telling Marilla about it, she repeated it all to Matthew. She knew that he loved to hear her talk.

"Well, I reckon it's going to be terrific," he said. "And you'll be great."

12

Merry Christmas

ACT IT OUT!

Marilla, Anne and Matthew are sitting together. There is a box in the middle of the floor.

Anne: Merry Christmas, Marilla! Merry Christmas, Matthew!

Matthew points to the box. Anne opens it up and pulls out a dress. She freezes.

Matthew: *(Worriedly)* Don't you like it?

Anne: Like it? Oh Matthew, it's exquisite. Look at those puffed sleeves!

Marilla: Well, yes. Pack it back in the box carefully, Anne. It's time for breakfast.

Anne: I'd rather feast my eyes on that dress! I will wear it to the concert this evening!

Anne leaves and comes back in wearing the dress. She twirls. Matthew looks delighted. Anne looks out of the window.

Anne: It's Diana!

Anne and Diana greeted each other with excitement, and Diana admired Anne's puffed sleeves. But there was no time to lose – they had to decorate the school hall and have one last rehearsal. They rushed to Avonlea school, laughing all the way.

That night, the hall was packed. In soft candlelight, the schoolchildren sang and performed their dance routines and everyone cheered. It was a most perfect evening. Anne and Diana walked home skipping and twirling beneath the dark, starry sky.

"Hasn't it been a brilliant evening?" Anne said, quite emotional. "Your solo was so elegant, Diana. I was so proud of you."

"And your recitals were brilliant, Anne. Everyone was transfixed by you."

"I was so nervous, but I just knew I had to be as dramatic as my puffed sleeves."

"Wasn't the boys' acting good?" Diana added. "Gilbert Blythe was—"

"I simply never waste a thought on him," Anne interrupted. And that was the end of that.

Diana and Anne said goodnight and went to their beds, and Marilla and Matthew sat by the kitchen fire a while, smiling. It was the first concert they had been to in twenty years.

"Our Anne did well tonight," Matthew said contentedly.

"Yes, she did," admitted Marilla. "I'm very proud of her, but I won't tell her. I don't want to spoil her."

"Well now, I was proud and I told her so just before she went upstairs."

Marilla took a long look at Matthew, who was distinctly misty-eyed.

"It won't be long before she outgrows Avonlea," he said. "We need to prepare for our girl's future."

13

Lessons

ACT IT OUT!

Diana and Anne are acting out a scene from a poem called 'The Lady of Shalott'. Anne is lying in a shallow rowing boat in the river. Diana is throwing flower petals over her.

Anne sits up suddenly.

Anne: I can feel water. Diana! I'm sinking!

Diana: Oh no! I'll get help!

Diana leaves. Anne clings onto the underside of a bridge. Gilbert rows by.

Gilbert: Anne Shirley, what are you doing?

Anne: *(Trying to be composed)* Well, if you must know, I was in Diana's rowing boat and it sprang a leak. Could you be so kind as to row me to the shore?

Gilbert rows her to shore. She gets out.

Anne: Thank you for your help, Mr Blythe.

Gilbert:	Now that I've rescued you, can we be friends?
Anne:	I shall never be friends with you, Gilbert Blythe.
Gilbert:	Fine! I'll never ask you again, Anne Shirley.

Gilbert rows away. Diana, Marilla and Rachel run to the lake.

Diana:	Oh, Anne. How did you escape?
Anne:	Gilbert Blythe rowed me to shore.
Diana:	What a hero! You'll have to speak to him after this, won't you?
Anne:	I certainly won't!

"Will you ever have any sense, Anne?" Marilla said, once they were back at Green Gables.

"Oh yes," Anne said brightly. "Every day I learn lessons from my mistakes."

"Such as?" Marilla challenged.

"Today's mistake will cure me of being too theatrical. From now on, I'm going to stop letting my imagination run away with me."

"I do hope so," Marilla said.

Matthew, who had been listening to the conversation, spoke up when Marilla left.

"Never give up on your imagination, Anne," he said. "A little of it every now and then is a wonderful thing."

One evening in November, Anne was reading on a rug by the fire.

"Anne, Miss Stacy was here this afternoon," Marilla said, softly.

"Why didn't you call me? Diana and I were just in the woods pretending it was haunted and scaring ourselves. Then we were thinking about the future. We promised that we will never get married, but instead be good friends who live together for ever."

"If you're more interested in the sound of your own voice, I won't bother telling you," grumbled Marilla.

"Oh please, Marilla, I'll be quiet. Go ahead."

Marilla explained that Miss Stacy wanted to hold study classes for students who she felt were smart enough to sit the entrance exam to Queen's College – a teacher training school. In her opinion, Anne was definitely good enough to go to the teaching school.

"Matthew and I have already agreed to fund any further education you need," Marilla said.

"It's been the dream of my life!" Anne yelped as she hugged Marilla.

Passing the exam became Anne's obsession. She put her imagination aside to concentrate on her studies. Her only sadness was for Diana, whose parents didn't believe in further education for girls. It was a tragedy, Anne thought. Diana was happy for Anne, though, and three weeks after Anne sat the exam, she arrived at Green Gables with news.

ACT IT OUT!

Diana hides a newspaper behind her back.

Anne: Oh Diana, it's been three whole weeks since the exams – I cannot stand the strain any longer.

Diana holds the paper out.

Diana: Anne, the results have been printed. You came joint first with Gilbert Blythe.

Anne snatches the paper.

Anne: I'm just dazzled inside!

Matthew: Well now, I always said you could beat them all easy.

Marilla: You've done well.

Matthew: I'm bursting with pride, Anne.

Anne flings her arms around her family.

14

Off to College

Anne left for Queen's College in a flurry of tears and dramatic speeches. Her absence also left a hole in the lives of her closest friends and family in Avonlea.

Matthew and Marilla often found themselves crying because they missed her. And while Diana tried to have fun with her other friends, there was no one quite like Anne.

Anne felt the same. She made friends – some even had imagination! – but she longed for Diana, and for Green Gables. It was only her dedication to study that kept her going – that, and her rivalry with Gilbert Blythe. They were neck and neck in everything, just as they had been at school.

At the end of the final term at college, Anne returned to Avonlea, her heart bursting with happiness. Diana was waiting for her on the porch of Green Gables to welcome her home.

ACT IT OUT!

Anne: It's just delicious being back! It's so good to see you, Diana.

They hug each other.

Diana: So, have you got your teaching certificate?

Anne: Oh yes. But I also won the Avery Award for best English student. It means I can go on to university! I should be excited, but I can't bear the thought of leaving Avonlea again.

Diana: University lasts for four years. I'll be old and grey when you come back!

Anne: Don't be silly! You'll be married to a handsome man by then, and you won't miss me at all.

Diana: Gilbert got the teaching job at Avonlea school, you know. His father can't afford any more education, so he's going to need to earn his way.

Anne: It's funny, I never spoke to Gilbert when we were at Queen's College together, but now I do think I was too hard on him. It's probably too late to ever be friends now.

Marilla and Matthew could barely conceal their joy at having Anne back, and Anne was happier than she'd been in a long time. However, she noticed a change in both of them. Marilla was looking tired, and Matthew was worryingly frail.

"He's had problems with his heart," Marilla confessed, when Anne asked. "But he won't stop working. He'll cheer up now you're home."

Anne ran outside right away and planted herself next to his side.

"You've been working too hard, Matthew," she said. "If I had been a boy, I'd have been able to help you in a hundred ways."

"Well now, I'd rather have you than a dozen boys, Anne," Matthew said. He smiled shyly, and Anne went back up to her room, where she watched him through the boughs of the Snow Queen, working down in the yard. It was the last time she would see him.

The very next morning, Matthew's fragile heart gave up.

A long, yawning sadness fell over Green Gables.

"Oh Marilla, what will we do without him?" Anne cried, and Marilla wrapped her arms around her and whispered:

"We've got each other, Anne. And I love you."

15

A Change of Heart

ACT IT OUT!

Marilla is sitting at the kitchen table looking solemn. Anne enters with flowers.

Marilla: Anne, someone has offered to buy Green Gables.

Anne drops her flowers.

Anne: But you can't sell Green Gables, you can't!

Marilla: I've been having trouble with my eyes and the doctor says I might lose my sight. Rachel has kindly said that I can live with her. I can't live here on my own when you go to university, Anne.

Anne: You won't have to stay here alone.

Marilla: What do you mean?

Anne: Let me tell you my plans. They need a teacher at Carmody school. I can ride back and forth and stay here – it's not far. We'll be really cosy here, you and I.

Marilla:	What about university? I won't allow you to sacrifice your education for me.
Anne:	It's no sacrifice, Marilla. And nothing could be worse than giving up Green Gables. I'm as stubborn as a mule so don't try to change my mind.
Marilla:	And I know better by now than to stand in your way. Thank you, Anne. Thank you.

News travelled fast as it often did in Avonlea, mostly thanks to Rachel Lynde. Soon, everyone knew that Anne had given up on university and was intending to teach instead. While some people thought she had made the wrong decision, others who knew her better understood – including Rachel. They sat, chatting together in the summer dusk, as the moths began to flit.

"I for one am glad you won't be cramming your head with Latin and Greek. It's not right for a girl," Rachel declared.

Anne laughed. "But I am going to study Latin and Greek. I'll do my university course at home in the evenings after I've been teaching at Carmody."

"Well," Rachel said with a know-all look. "I think you'll actually be teaching at Avonlea school."

"No, Gilbert Blythe has that job," Anne corrected.

"He did. But when he heard about your decision, he took a job at White Sands so you can have the Avonlea teaching post."

"I can't let him do that!" Anne exclaimed, her heart racing.

"The papers are already signed."

Anne was stunned. And Rachel Lynde looked at her much like Marilla did nowadays – with a great deal of affection.

The following evening, Anne went to the graveyard with flowers for Matthew's grave. She stayed there until the sun began to set, talking to Matthew and looking out over the clover fields.

She was taking her time walking home when she came across Gilbert. He nodded his head politely and turned away but Anne saw this was her chance to put things right.

ACT IT OUT!

Anne: Gilbert, stop! Why did you give up your job for me?

Gilbert: I knew how much being able to stay at Green Gables with Marilla would mean to you.

Anne: It's so kind of you. I don't know how to thank you.

Gilbert: It isn't all out of kindness. I was hoping this small gesture would mean we could be friends. Anne, can you finally forgive me?

Anne: *(Laughing)* Goodness, I was such a stubborn old goose, Gilbert. I forgave you the day you rescued me from sinking in Diana's boat, but I never said so. I've regretted it ever since.

Gilbert: We were born to be the best of friends, admit it. Perhaps we can help each other with our studies – I plan to keep up with them, don't you?

Anne: Yes. And I promise not to break a slate over your head.

Gilbert: Come on, Anne of Green Gables. I'll walk you home.

Anne: *(To herself)* Yes, I am Anne of Green Gables, and I am perfectly happy at last.

The End

Now answer the questions …

1 What does Anne decide to call Barry's Pond when she first arrives in Avonlea?

2 Why does Anne hit Gilbert over the head with her slate?

3 What does Anne mean when she uses the word 'tragic' in Chapters 2 and 5?

4 Explain what Anne's childhood was like before she arrived in Green Gables.

5 How could Anne tell who the gift of a strawberry apple was from when she returned to school, and why did she drop it on the floor?

6 Explain how Rachel's feelings towards Matthew and Marilla taking in an orphan change. What does Anne do to change Rachel's opinion of her?

7 Anne tells Matthew: "Red hair will be my lifelong sorrow." Find two examples from the story which prove how sensitive Anne is about people mentioning her hair.

8 Which character from the story did you feel you had the most in common with? Explain why, using words and phrases from the story to support your answer.